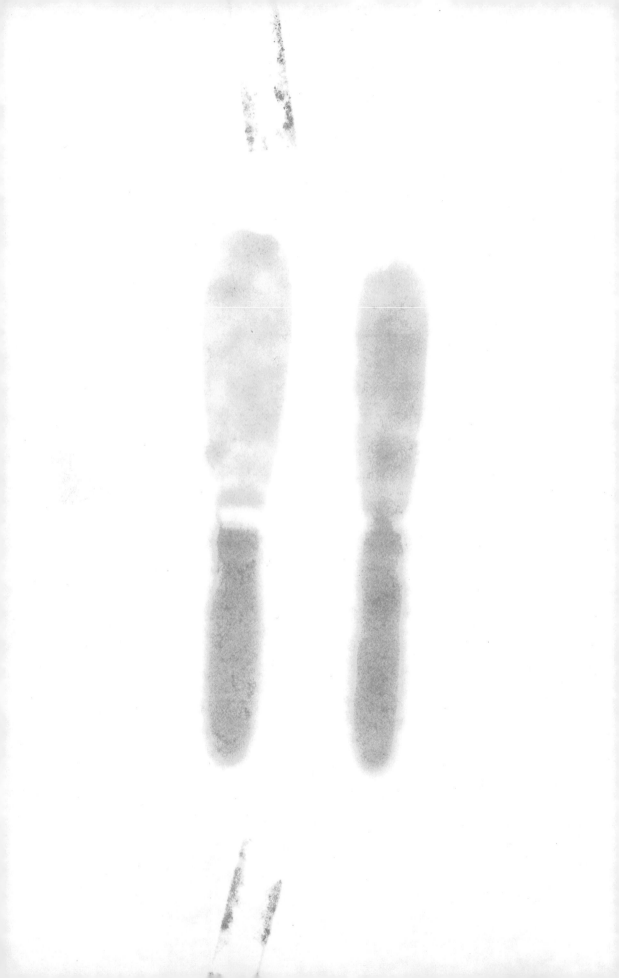

THE NEW VISIONS

THE NEW VISIONS

A COLLECTION OF MODERN SCIENCE FICTION ART

Introduction by Frederik Pohl

Doubleday & Company, Inc.
Garden City, New York

INTRODUCTION

Shortly after my novel *Gateway* was published, I was drafted for an autographing session at a science fiction convention in Tucson, Arizona. This sort of thing goes on all the time at science fiction conventions. Readers seem to like it well enough, and of course the authors are tickled pink—once a book is autographed, you see, it can no longer be returned for refund. So the convention authorities set me up at a table, one of half a dozen in a large room, and a line of readers began to file up with their books to be signed. There was another person signing books about a yard away. I nodded to him as we both began, but I remember thinking it rather odd that I didn't recognize him—there are several hundred science fiction writers in the United States, but we mostly know each other well enough. Nonetheless I didn't think about it very much because (I am happy to report) business was pretty brisk. About half an hour later I caught a glimpse, out of the corner of my eye, of *what* this person was autographing.

He was autographing copies of my novel *Gateway*. What's more, there were as many people in his line as in mine.

Now, what do you suppose the etiquette books advise in a case like that? There must be some appropriate action, but I could not think what it was. I considered bribing one of the fans to cry, "Will the real Fred Pohl please stand up?" I thought of calling a member of the convention committee, or even, wildly, of inviting this impostor to step outside—that shows how disoriented I was, because he was in a lot better shape than I was. Fortunately, it didn't come to that. There was a lull just about then. The fellow turned my way, smiled and introduced himself. He had painted the dust jacket for the book, and so had every right to be autographing it; and that's how I first met Boris Vallejo.

I certainly agree it makes as much sense to get an artist's autograph as an author's. I always have thought so—Boris just caught me unawares. When I first discovered science fiction, I knew at once that the next best thing to reading it was poring over the pictures that went with the stories.

There were plenty of pictures, too. Not many science fiction stories appeared in book form in the 1930s. Science fiction came in magazines—mostly pulp magazines. Some of them were bedsheet sized, some small, but every one of them was lavishly illustrated. At least one black-and-white line drawing for every story, and always a four-color painting on the cover.

It has to be said that some of the art wasn't very good. (Some of the stories weren't, either.) But a lot of it was really beautiful, and all of it was fun.

The dean of artists of science fiction, for the first decade that there was such a thing as science fiction, was a man named Frank R. Paul. Paul's specialty was creating machines—great, rotating, cogwheeled, monstrous machines; his machines were far more handsome than his human beings. He would have done well illustrating patent applications, and as a matter of fact, Paul came to Hugo Gernsback's magazine *Amazing Stories* from Gernsback's other publications, which were mostly in the areas of science, invention, and home hobbyists. Paul was so eminent in his field that he was chosen as Guest of Honor at the very first World Science Fiction Convention in 1939. But by then he was beginning to have challengers for the crown: Virgil Finlay, who produced beautiful human figures and exquisite alien scenes, with every tiny detail painstakingly drawn in; Hubert Rogers, whose craggy-featured "Lensmen" illustrated Doc Smith's great series; Chesley Bonestell, the finest astronomical painter ever—he graduated to do the space scenes for the film *Destination Moon*, and his astro-murals, notably the one in the Boston planetarium, are still on view; Leydenfrost; Wesso; Hannes Bok; Elliott Dold; later on Ed Emshwiller and the whole batch of *Galaxy* artists—there were dozens of them, and each one had painfully evolved his own individual style.

I do not say that the science fiction artists of the thirties, forties, and fifties were better than today's crop—it wouldn't be true—but they had an advantage. There was more art to do then. With the magazine census depleted and most books limited to a single piece of art on the dust jacket, there's less to look at than there used to be—which is just one of the reasons why this book is such a good idea. (There are a couple of dozen other reasons inside, and to find them, all you have to do is turn the pages.)

The artist who commits himself to science fiction takes on a formidable job. He has to make a picture of something that has never yet existed. He has no model or "swipe file" to help him. If he is illustrating an actual story, it is tougher yet. He has to give form to an airy imagining—and not even his own imagining, at that, but that of the author of the story. Authors are not always helpful to their artists. Sometimes what they write about is well described, but more often authors use the kind of words that evoke an image for a reader but don't do a thing for the draftsman. (How do you make a picture of "a blackness blacker than black"?)

To deal with these problems, every good artist has to evolve his own strategies—often a selection of strategies, different attacks to meet different problems. Sometimes the best thing to do is to paint with utter realism, as close to a Kodachrome as brush and canvas can get. Sometimes the essential meat of the story can't be shown, and can only be suggested; other times, the very best thing an artist can do is throw away the writer's attempts at being visual-minded and invent an appropriate fantasy of his own. Sounds hard? It *is* hard—but the twenty-three artists in this book stand as proof that it can be done.

I wish I could say something about each one of them—even about each painting; but what I have to say is less interesting in this book than what they have to show you. Even so, I must record my pleasure at seeing Ken Barr's and Ed Valigursky's works, Richard Corben's stately alien castle and his Jurassic big-game hunter, and David K. Stone's cocky *Stainless Steel Rat*— And Richard Powers' wonderful abstraction; he graced the covers of a lot of books of mine years ago, and astonished me when, visiting a gallery on 57th Street once, I found a whole one-man Powers' show of lovely monochromes of New England fishing villages. I also delight in Boris Vallejo's rendering of Gordon Dickson's *The Dragon and the George*. (Unfortunately, the painting of a spaceship Boris was autographing in Arizona isn't included as well; this volume features only artwork that was originally commissioned for the Science Fiction Book Club.)

Gary Viskupic's paintings also have personal memories for me: my own youthful fan's excitement at *Slan;* the days when I was literary agent for Clifford Simak and John Wyndham, and *City* and *The Day of the Triffids* were new; a few years later, the writing of *The Starchild Trilogy* with Jack Williams; later still the sad but rewarding task of putting together those wonderful stories in *The Best of C. M. Kornbluth*—

But those are just my own personal memories. There's plenty here for everyone, so turn the page and start evoking your own!

Frederik Pohl

EDITORS' NOTE

This collection of outstanding science fiction artwork highlights a wide spectrum of jacket art commissioned over the years for Doubleday's Science Fiction Book Club.

To accompany these paintings, the featured artists graciously agreed to render self-portraits and provide brief biographical notes about their art background and interest in science fiction. As is evident, each artist responded to our request for this information in his own way. The result: verbal and visual self-portraits of 23 noted illustrators, and 46 striking color paintings that capture the distinctive and impressive styles of individuals whose work has graced the covers of countless science fiction book jackets and appeared in many other artistic media.

The paintings in this collection were chosen as representative of the wide range of techniques and imagination that characterize modern science fiction art. We hope that you'll find these paintings of distant planets, spaceships, alien cities, and the aliens themselves an exciting visual treat.

MARY SHERWIN
ELLEN ASHER
JOE MILLER

Frank Frazetta

Born in Brooklyn, New York, Frank Frazetta discovered the wonders of drawing before he was three years old. With his family's interest and encouragement, he continued his drawings through those early years and was enrolled at the Brooklyn Academy of Fine Arts when he was eight. In his midteens, as an assistant to science fiction cartoonist John Giunta, Frazetta persuaded Giunta to include a character and story he had created eight years earlier (called "Snowman") in the premier issue of *Tally-Ho Comics*, December 1944.

Frank Frazetta continued working for a variety of comic publishers until 1950, when his own comic, called "Thun'da, King of the Congo" was published. Then came his acclaimed series of Buck Rogers cover illustrations and a syndicated newspaper strip titled "Johnny Comet." In 1954 Al Capp invited Frazetta to join the staff working on the "Li'l Abner" comic; he stayed on for nine years.

In 1964 Frazetta turned his interests to paperback covers, preparing artwork for Edgar Rice Burroughs' novels and the best-selling Conan series by Robert E. Howard. Other accomplishments over the years include four volumes of his own artwork, three calendars, and over a hundred posters.

"An Artist is one who is creative, original, and paints from the heart with honesty and conviction," Frazetta says. Priding himself on his creativeness and totally original concepts, he once stated, "I could do anything I wanted as long as I did it well."

Frank Frazetta is currently in California, coproducing an animated film with Ralph Bakshi. His family includes his wife, Eleanor, and four children.

Richard Corben

Richard Corben, born in Missouri and raised in Kansas, knew at an early age that he wanted to be an artist. His parents recognized his talent but were skeptical about art as a career. Nevertheless they sent him to the Kansas City Art Institute where he excelled in the studio courses. This art training and his amateur animated films enabled him to get a job in the art department of an industrial film company in Kansas City. While working there during the day, he continued his related interests of comics and painting in the evening.

During this time Richard Corben discovered the possibilities for science fiction and fantasy artwork, and as a result, he began submitting his illustrations to comic and science fiction magazines. The volume of his work on comics eventually grew to such an extent that he quit his film job to begin a full-time free-lance career. He also worked on several science fiction assignments, as well as some magazine covers and a record album cover.

In the last few years he has done extensive work on book covers, record albums, and film-advertising posters, and barely has time to work on his comic series. Richard Corben's work is also popular in Europe where his comics *Bloodstar*, *Den*, and *New Tales of the Arabian Nights* have found a new audience.

The 1977 Annual World's Best SF
edited by Donald A. Wollheim

Tony Gleeson

Mission of Gravity,
by Hal Clement

It's really difficult to describe how my work gets done: when things are going right, the piece just sort of draws or paints *itself* and I wind up with something very different from my original conception. It can be downright frightening! The hardest job, on my part, is usually to relax and stay out of its way in the process.

I grew up on fantasy and science fiction and learned to read from comic books, which may explain my lifelong love for the genre and the fundamental weirdness which people seem to find in even my most straightforward work. Since moving to Los Angeles in 1977, I have become involved in a wide variety of projects—not only science fiction but also painting for exhibitions and all manner of illustration and graphic design. I'm often faced with a whole spectrum of problems to solve; sometimes disconcerting, but almost always rewarding.

The more sane—oftentimes the crazier—part of my life is shared with my wife Annie and our two kids, Matt and Alexandra. Friends sometimes ask if they're going to be artists like Dad or go into medicine like Mom. My guess is that they'll probably shock us both and do something as bizarre and unorthodox as becoming lawyers or stock brokers . . .

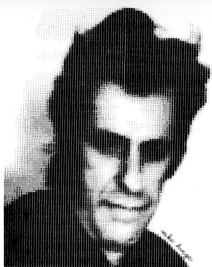

Mike Hinge

Work to favorite New Wave groups: Ultravox, Joy Division, and Orchestral Manoeuvres in the Dark, etc., on headphones. Training on violin, playing trombone at age eighteen at Teachers Training College. Hung around after hours at music and dance club to take turns learning how to play double bass. Liked the sound effect of horns; played a B-flat Besson trumpet.

Father born in England, mother in Africa, first of father's family to be born in Polynesia. Childhood spent on a dairy farm cut out of virgin rain forest. At a fine-arts academy studied still life, drapery, and drawing from plaster casts. Seddon Memorial Polytechnic, woodwork, applied mechanics, architectural drawing, etc. Introduction to H. G. Wells, pyrotechnics, and modern music.

From working at biggest ad agency in New Zealand to "Art Center College of Design," Los Angeles, studied illustration, design and rendering. Fashion layouts, May Co. and J. C. Penney; supermarket interiors and graphics, Brand-Worth; lighting and fixture design, Feldman Co.; first 16mm movie (b&w, unfinished); drawing first art-nouveau-influenced psychedelic works, first poster

©1979 mike hinge

printed 1962.

Moved to New York in 1966. Art director for ad agencies Y&R and B.B.D.&O., two awards in the 13th Type Directors show. Designed alphabets, Hinge computer—electronic, robot, quasar, integrated and digital readout, for Photo Lettering. Worked with TV art director on second 16mm color film titled *City*, built a small kinetic sculpture for the film; joined "EAT," Engineers, Artists and Technology; "Some New Beginnings," Brooklyn Museum catalog. Onyx display, Wittenborn bookstore; rendering exhibition, Architectural League, New York; poster in "time capsule" of Oakland Museum, California. Cryobionic unit designed for film *2001: A Space Odyssey.*

Painting of Hirohito, Emperor of Japan, for *Time*, exhibited in Europe and the Middle East, portrait gallery collection, Smithsonian Museum. Nixon "The Push to Impeach" cover for *Time*, both paintings on TV. Co-exhibitor, Quatre Artistes Contemporains in 1979, Centre Culturel Americain Paris. Published in *Heavy Metal.*

Masters of Everon,
by Gordon R. Dickson

Larry Kresek

As a free-lance illustrator, Larry Kresek has worked in various areas of the publishing industry, and his illustrations have appeared in many books and magazines. Other projects include a series of pharmaceutical illustrations and other medically related artwork, advertising, and movie illustrations.

Aside from his practical experience as an illustrator, Larry Kresek has studied painting at the Art Center College of Design in Los Angeles, the University of Delaware, and in Europe. His paintings are included in private collections throughout the United States and in many group shows in the New York metropolitan area.

"What is science fiction anyway? I've never been able to understand who makes up these artificial distinctions that place Andy Warhol over here, Andy Wyeth over there, and Vinnie Van Gogh way, way over there.

"These divisions of convenience just get in the way and painting is painting and sometimes painting is good. It used to be that if there was a rocket ship and a fellow with a fishbowl over his head, wow, that was science fiction! Not anymore . . ."

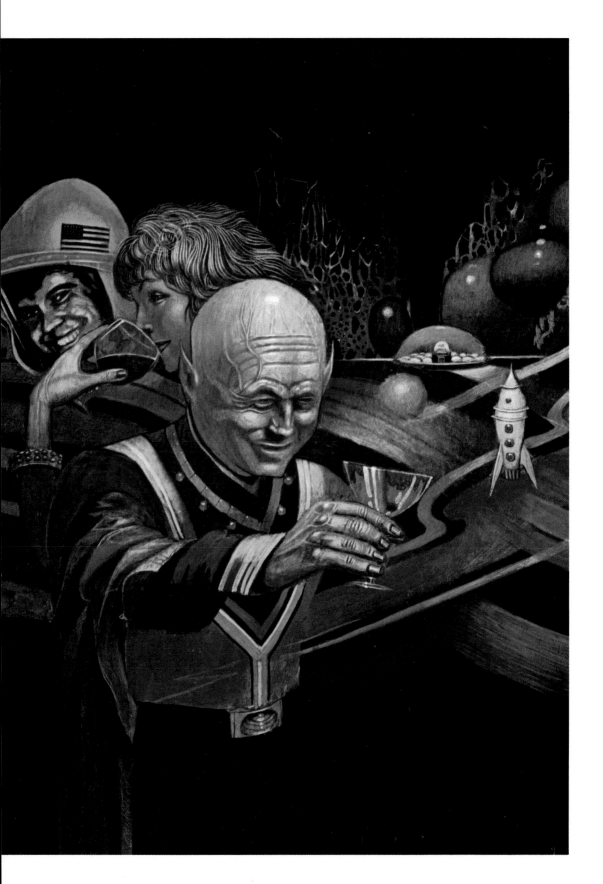

The Seven Deadly Sins of Science Fiction
edited by Isaac Asimov, Charles G. Waugh, and Martin H. Greenberg

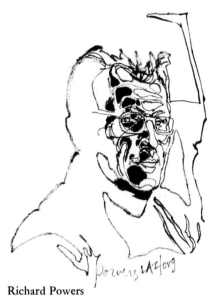

Richard Powers

When I (hereinafter, he) was a child, shortly after the Black Sox scandal of the end of the second decade of this century, a scandal which shaped subsequent events of the same century just as surely as the invention of emphysema, he was blessed with a recurrent nightmare during the course of which the inside of his head, a pulsing polyglobism with a texture similar to that of tapioca, only smarter, grew larger and larger until it outgrew the confines of his small blond skull; the brain became the confines, and the skull, the encompassed . . . a swelling yeasty heaving independently tapioca sentience . . . dreadful trauma for a sensitive little chap.

Inevitably, however, a career in science fiction followed and some four hundred to five hundred science fiction covers.

Richard Powers was born in Chicago, Illinois, in the best month of 1921. He was irreparably educated in Jesuit institutions before attending the Art Institute of Chicago, the University of Illinois Fine Arts School (on a football scholarship), the Mizen Academy of Art, the U. S. Army (four refreshingly unaesthetic years thereof), the New School for Social Research (New York), the Art School thereof, the Jay Connaway School of Marine and Landscape Painting in Monhegan Island, Maine, and in Dorset, Vermont.

He paints exclusively in acrylic, freehand, after preliminary yoga exercises.

He is married to a ruthless young tennis professional and resides in Ridgefield, Connecticut, where he has had his working studio for some twenty-five years.

The 1978 Annual World's Best SF,
edited by Donald A. Wollheim

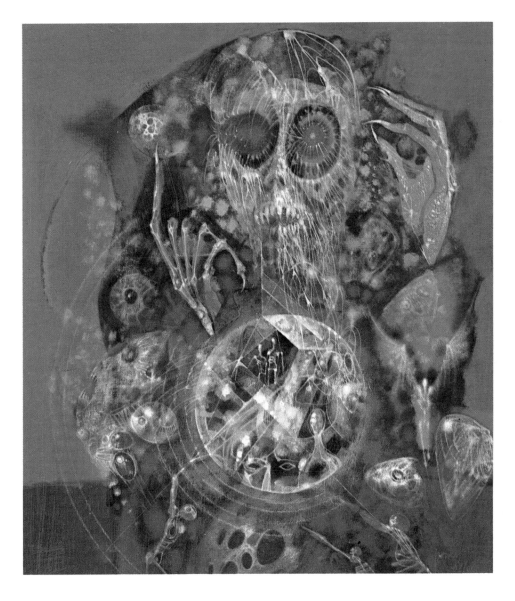

David K. Stone

DavKarl Stone was born in Reedsport,
Oregon, and studied art at the University of
Oregon, Art Center College at Los Angeles,
and the Universidad de Michoacan in Mexico.
His art career has included a wide variety of illustrations
for books, advertising, and magazines. (Stone's science
fiction work began with *Galaxy* magazine.) He has
designed several commemorative stamps for the U. S.
Postal Service. In another specially commissioned project,
lasting three and a half years, he painted seventy portraits
of the members of the International Aerospace Hall of
Fame.

David Stone's paintings hang in many permanent and
private art collections, including those of the U. S. Air
Force, the Smithsonian Institution, and the Society of
Illustrators, of which he is a former president. He is the
recipient of a number of art awards and has traveled
around the world on art assignments. His family includes
his wife, Peggy, and two daughters, Kelly and Jamie.

"Whenever I draw a subject such as a building or a
face, its details remain in my memory for a long time. It's
the same with illustrating a story. Five years ago I
completed the *Mission to Moulokin* painting, but its
jagged world of ice and the leonine Sir Hunnar Redbeard
are clear in my mind. I shall never forget the tall warrior
of the *Faded Sun* tales and his squat, scuttling enemies of
Kesrith, nor the fearsome, faithful beast of Kutath. James
Bolivar diGriz remains unforgettable because of his
dinosaur suit.

"These details were selected at the time to set the tone,
the unique nature of that particular novel. While my
pencil roamed the sketch pad, the characters slowly
emerged. Sometimes they were born from the author's
descriptions or simply from the situations in which they
were placed, but always from a massive stretch of my
imagination.

"Although most science fiction calls for extraterrestrial
humanoids, unworldly creatures, and I may falter from a
shortage of imagination to portray a tough one, a short
walk down a busy New York street will provide me with
enough models for the most fantastic yarns."

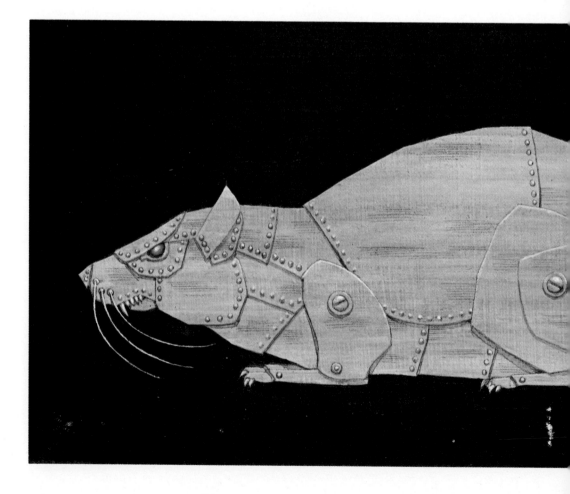

33

The Faded Sun: Kesrith,
by C. J. Cherryh

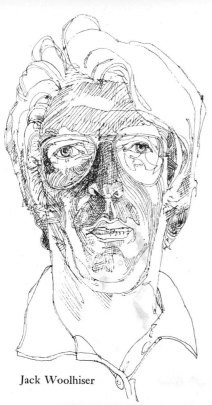

Jack Woolhiser

Inspired by his artist father, Jack Woolhiser studied at New York's prestigious Pratt Institute, thereafter establishing his reputation as one of the country's most respected free-lance artists. Woolhiser's paintings and illustrations have appeared in leading national magazines and are featured in many private collections. He particularly enjoys science fiction illustrations because of his fascination for spaceships and the imagination and creativity they require. Born in New York, Jack Woolhiser is married and the father of four children.

"I remember reading *Amazing Stories*, *Astounding*, and *Analog* magazines years ago and being intrigued not only by the writing in these publications, but by the remarkable illustrations of Chesley Bonestell. His almost photographic technique rendered sweeping and soaring mountainscapes with dramatic precision. In retrospect, they were much more exciting than the drab rolling hills visited by the Apollo astronauts decades later . . .

"In science fiction, the artist has a sense of freedom that is not matched by any other form of realistic commercial art. I find it extremely exciting because of the possibilities. Your color sense is probed and unleashed; wild swirls can become galaxies; supernovas and spaceships become huge horizontal cities built layer upon layer.

"A combination of the real and unreal often produces wonderful things—human clones to androids to winged insects that are alien spaceships . . . the possibilities are endless, exciting, and always changing.

"The illustrations of today have come a long way since the time of Mr. Bonestell. Perhaps it's the many discoveries that science seems to give us daily. Who would have imagined the possibility, for example, that things like black holes existed! It's almost like Lewis Carroll's White Queen who always made it a practice to imagine six impossible things before breakfast. What lies ahead is perhaps the best question."

The Faded Sun: Shon'Jir,
by C. J. Cherryh

Three from the Legion
by Jack Williamson

Ed Valigursky

Ed Valigursky has won numerous awards for his artwork, including the Gold Medal Award from the Association of Industrial Artists. He has paintings on permanent exhibit in the Pentagon, and several naval and air force installations.

"My first science fiction illustrations were done while I attended the Art Institute of Pittsburgh. Two of these illustrations were later submitted and sold to *Fantastic Adventures*, a Ziff-Davis publication. Subsequently I became a monthly contributor to their science fiction magazines and then Associate Art Director.

"In 1954, after leaving Ziff-Davis, I began devoting myself entirely to free-lance illustration. At first, my designs were mostly science fiction covers for magazines and paperbacks, and then illustrations of aircraft and marine stories for such magazines as *Saga*, *Argosy*, and *True*. Other projects included a tremendous amount of advertising illustration, some of a science fiction nature.

"At present my science fiction illustration, unfortunately, represents only a small percentage of my work—mostly paperback covers, advertising illustration, and regular contributions to *Popular Mechanics* magazine.

"My goal is to devote myself entirely to oil painting, primarily marine and aircraft subjects. I have taken my first step toward that goal by recently becoming a member of the Society of American Historical Artists.

"If I ever completely leave the illustration field, I will do so with a great deal of sadness. My first love will always be designing machines for science fiction illustration."

Victor Valla

Victor Valla's interest and commitment to an illustration career began when he was about ten years old. He received degrees in Painting, Illustration, and Printmaking from the Rochester Institute of Technology and the University of Illinois. Following a year of teaching at RIT, he was awarded a grant to study in Paris at the famous Printmaking Workshop of Stanley Hayter.

Victor Valla has received many illustration awards and for two consecutive years received Gold Medals for illustration from the Art Directors Club of New Jersey. He presently teaches graphic design and illustration at Kean College of New Jersey in Union.

"For several years I have worked in a combination of inks, dyes, airbrush, and casein, often with collage elements; also, on canvas and board.

"For the painting reproduced here, I was trying to somehow personify the two characters and make clear the differences in their character by the manner in which they were depicted. As I often do, I tried to 'cast' them as movie or TV characters to see who might play the 'types' in question—I arrived at Jack Palance and Wally Cox after some discussion with the art director.

"When I work on other types of science fiction such as Lovecraft books, I try to capture the *mood* of the stories or novel. This requires symbolism and color choices, but most importantly, spacial definition in order to create a context. Not space as 'outer space' necessarily, but space as near, far, surreal, otherworldly, futuristic, contradictory, spacial tensions, multiple spaces.

"To me, if one can create a feeling of dread, gloom, anxiety, conflict, depression, awe, or danger by other than obvious symbols or literal images, the whole tone of the book or story is conveyed, and thus the impact the author had in mind can better be reached for. That, for me, is the challenge of science fiction art."

The 1974 Annual World's Best SF,
edited by Donald A. Wollheim

Boris W. Vallejo

BORIS -77

Boris Vallejo's formal training began at the age of fourteen with evening classes at the Escuela Nacional de Bellas Artes in Peru. At the time he had no intention of pursuing an art career—hardly a lucrative profession in Peru. Rather, his involvement with art was a matter of love—love of being able to interpret what he saw and felt and thought through the medium of a pencil and a sketch pad. Even before these lessons, he practiced drawing movie stars whose sharp, dramatically lit photographs were readily available. This developed his eye for proportion, contrast, and effective use of light and shadow.

"More than anything else I am impressed by skill," he says. "To illustrate is to tell a story. One should be able to do this, to convey the message by means of a skilled technique, not simply by emotional paint slapping. This is what separates the talented dilettante from the talented professional." A lack of technique, he observes, can be faked and nevertheless impress the untrained eye. "This is not to say that everything in a painting must be sharp or important. But what is not, what is secondary, should be minimized with control.

"To rise above the mediocre, one's drawing skill must first and foremost be second nature. Proportion and perspective must no longer present problems. Good drawing is the foundation of all excellent art; and then the control of the medium—oil, acrylics, watercolors, whatever.

"No matter how much talent you have, you can't develop it to its fullest extent if you are on the lookout for shortcuts. The most important motivation for doing any creative work must be the love you have for it. How difficult it is, how much time it will take, how much actual work is involved—all this is secondary and should be (barring a very concrete deadline) disregarded.

"The finished painting should hold all the excitement of discovery and creation that any dedicated artist needs."

The World of Tiers (Volume 1),
by Philip José Farmer

Ken Barr

Born in Glasgow, Scotland, Ken Barr began his career at the age of fourteen by serving six years as an apprentice sign painter. After his apprenticeship and a two-year hitch with the British Army in North Africa, he moved to London, where he worked in various studios and advertising agencies, expanding his experience and skills in every area of commercial art.

In 1967 Barr emigrated to the United States, continuing a free-lance career begun in the United Kingdom in 1958, mainly in the field of comic books, men's adventure magazines, paperback book covers, and movie posters.

Always particularly fond of science fiction and fantasy in any form, whether it be novels, movies, or comic books, he painted his first science fiction cover for *Nebula* (a British science fiction magazine published by fellow Scot, Peter Hamilton) in 1958. Soon he found that science fiction and fantasy art freed and developed the imagination in a way not otherwise possible within the restrictions of commercial art.

Although best known for his work in science fiction, fantasy, and what he calls "gothic classic," Ken Barr maintains a strong reputation in advertising art, cartooning, and design. Not surprisingly, his favorite authors include Ray Bradbury, Roger Zelazny, Alfred Bester, Andre Norton, and others who contrive to write so descriptively that work becomes easy and pleasurable for illustrators.

Michael Whelan

T hroughout my childhood my family moved
approximately every one and a half years to a
different town in California or Colorado. Since I
spent a lot of time being the "new kid" in the
neighborhood and didn't have any friends, I turned to
reading and art. I credit this and the fact that my father is
an aerospace engineer as key factors in my development. I
also loved going to corny science fiction and horror movies
that were in such abundance in the 1950s. As I recall, some
of the first words I learned to read were from lurid ads in
the newspapers for a monster movie! But even before I
could read, I enjoyed looking at covers of science fiction
books and magazines we had around the house. From early
on I took a shine to the visual matter of science fiction and
fantasy, and I would try to draw my versions of the scenes
in the movies and books. In many cases my drawings
would help me to win new friends—it still seems to work.

As insistent as my interest in science fiction and fantasy
was, it wasn't until my senior year at San Jose State
University that I seriously considered illustration as a
career. Until then I felt that I had to have a "real job" and
planned on being a doctor or biologist. I even took a
number of pre-med courses before changing my mind.
This turned out to be a great advantage, for it gave me a
solid basis for the study of the human figure. Thanks to
those classes and my three-year job in the anatomy-
physiology department as "cadaver-preparer," model-
maker, and medical illustrator, I have a great groundwork
from which I can extrapolate in constructing alien life
forms.

After graduating from college with a BA in painting
and as a President's Scholar, I went to the Art Center
College of Design in Los Angeles to polish up my
professional skills. Upon receiving offers of work on the
East Coast, I moved there, and have since created over 130
book cover paintings, as well as magazine, record album,
and other art.

Whether I am illustrating a fantasy/science fiction story
or visualizing something from the world around us, the
communication of a "sense of wonder" is the essential
motivation for each painting. Also, it is especially
important for an illustrator to communicate some of the
content (emotional, thematic, whatever) of the written
work. If the artwork doesn't do this, it fails as an
illustration. Thus, the greatest reward for me as an
illustrator comes when I feel I've succeeded on both
counts: communicating the essence of what has been
written and promoting a sense of wonder.

Gary Viskupic

Pursuing an interest in science fiction, Gary Viskupic has provided illustrations for numerous book covers and promotional pieces for the Science Fiction Book Club over the years. He has executed this work in pen and ink with watercolor overlays or Dr. Martin's dyes and, more recently, has begun the use of acrylics. Using these media to illustrate subject matter that has always fascinated him, he has produced "far-out" images that figuratively "blow one's mind into the far reaches of space."

Growing up in the 1950s, Viskupic was influenced by the sci-fi movies of the era, particularly *The Invasion of the Body Snatchers* and *It Came from Outer Space.*

In the hours when he is not creating conceptual art for the op-ed pages of *Newsday*, Gary Viskupic is turning out voluminous work free-lance for clients that range from *Psychology Today* and *Business Week* to the Washington *Post.* He is equally active in poster design.

Viskupic's awards are numerous and include recognition by the Art Directors Club of New York, *Graphis Poster Annual*, *Graphis Annual*, and *Modern Publicity*. His work has been exhibited in international shows in Japan, England, France, and Czechoslovakia, as well as the Bicentennial Poster Exhibition sponsored by the Smithsonian Institution. A major article on his work appeared in *Print Magazine* in 1975.

City,
by Clifford D. Simak

Slan,
by A. E. van Vogt

The Day of the Triffids,
by John Wyndham

John Berkey

John Berkey's interest in painting began while he was in high school. After graduation he attended a Minneapolis art school and subsequently got a job at a commercial studio. Over the years Berkey has worked on a wide range of projects: impressionistic space art, historical scenes for calendars, pastoral landscapes, advertising art, and motion picture posters. He lives in a quiet Minnesota town with his wife and children, and paints at home in a basement studio.

"The words *Science* and *Fiction* have always seemed to me to be opposites. Science, a proven fact based on search; and fiction, an idea extending from reality. In painting Science Fiction I have always tried to work toward the illusion of both. A combination of painted believable space plus how to see the written and imagined ideas within that space. It perhaps could be said that most illustration is a form of this combination. Science Fiction offers the unique chance to paint and then to see. The work also is a pleasant opposite from seeing and then painting."

Tony Fiyalko

Tony Fiyalko is a native of New York City and makes his home on Long Island with his wife, Kathy. He is a graduate of the School of Visual Arts and his work has appeared in the New York *Times*, *Retail Week*, *Newsday*, and in various children's books and publications.

"I don't generally think of myself as a science fiction artist since I tend to shy away from the technological realism that I've always felt is the mark of true science fiction art. My style (a blend of watercolors, pastels, and color pencils) is much softer and understated. I'll leave the hardware to those with more scientific imaginations and techniques. However, my work does have a natural inclination toward the bizarre and an off-center sense of humor that lends itself to the genre.

"I'd love to do more science fiction and fantasy illustrations for children's stories. Kids have fertile imaginations and voracious appetites for such stuff. I can recall hoarding and poring over stacks of digest-sized sci-fi magazines when I was a kid. The gorgeous cover paintings, by illustrators like Kelly Freas and Ed Emshwiller, fired my enthusiasm even more than the stories within. If my work could ever have such an effect on some youngster, I'd be most gratified."

The Magic of Xanth,
by Piers Anthony

Tony Hyalke

The Long Afternoon of Earth,
by Brian Aldiss

Fancies and Goodnights,
by John Collier

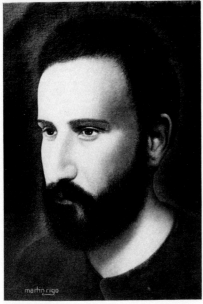

Martin Rigo

Martin Rigo was born in Barcelona in 1949, where he received a general education and later attended the School of Art.

From the very beginning, his goal was to become a painter. This was his father's profession, and as a child Martin became familiar with the world of canvases, watercolors, oils, brushes, etc., and was fascinated by the idea of transforming a canvas' white emptiness into something beautiful.

At age seventeen he went to work for a scientific publishing house, where he spent five years illustrating works on human anatomy, physics, biology, astronomy, etc. These years of practice enabled him to acquire extensive experience with oils and great skill in producing the high-precision illustrations required for scientific texts.

At the same time, he worked to develop his pictorial side, in connection with important art galleries. His works have been shown in Barcelona, Alicante, Madrid, Valencia, Santander, Paris, Prague, and other European cities. He has also participated in various national art contests, winning a number of prizes.

His pictures have always reflected man's relationship to his natural environment: water, earth, vegetation, animals. "Nowadays, however, after so many great scientific discoveries and technological advances, man's environment is not just the Earth, but the entire solar system, toward which we've taken giant strides through space flights and most recently the success of the space shuttle Columbia. For this reason, fantasy and science fiction art have become increasingly popular. They have the power to make us see other worlds and ways of life, which perhaps aren't so far from our own."

Martin Rigo has worked as a science fiction and fantasy illustrator, although he feels more identified with the latter category.

At present, his work appears regularly in international magazines, as well as on book covers of leading European and American publishing houses.

Les Katz

Circus World,
by Barry B. Longyear

By the age of twelve I had seen Frazetta's "Conan" and E. R. Burroughs' paperback jackets and decided that illustrating was the way I wanted to make a living. I also spent much time devouring *Marvel Comics*, which I still enjoy today for their sense of pacing, design, and dramatics.

My formal art education began in 1972 at the University of Bridgeport where I studied Industrial Design. There I was taught the very basic drawing principles of form, spacial relationships, and perspective. The designing exercises we were given taught us problem-solving, which helps not only in creating functional toasters and can openers but science fiction book jackets as well.

A few more years were spent at The School of Visual Arts in New York, wrenching knowledge from several top illustrators/teachers and studying basic painting, design, and assorted techniques. After leaving school, I spent six months putting together a portfolio and then went out to seek my fortune. I'm still seeking it.

My approach to all assignments, science fiction included, is to read the manuscript and look for the central themes or images that convey the essentials of the book. I then design several sketches—illustrating the various ideas I've come up with. I've found my picture file (three five-drawer legal file cabinets containing twenty-five hundred picture categories) to be an invaluable tool in doing my work. Sometimes a strange shot or something taken totally out of context will set off an image for me to elaborate on. This evolves into the sketch.

When I begin a painting, I start with a tight pencil rendering of an approved sketch and then complete the work in acrylics. At times I may use pastels, crayons, and inks—whatever technique serves the purpose best. I always try to go beyond "standard" science fiction imagery, opting instead for as offbeat a solution as possible while still being true to the book. The wonderful juxtaposition of fantasy and reality found in really good science fiction allows me to be as creative and imaginative as I can.

Esteban Maroto

I was born in Madrid, a city lost in the outermost
reaches of the galaxy. Almost at once I realized that
many things had to change, but . . . I also noticed
that I didn't have what it took to change them—
money, intelligence, skill, willpower, and a great deal
more. I learned that some things were unchangeable
and in other cases one had to make the effort. But like I
said, I didn't have the wit to distinguish them; and that's
how I've spent most of my life, fighting a sometimes
absurd battle.

In the midst of all this mess, there was one world where
I always found delight: fantasy, within which,
paradoxically, I discovered my own reality. There's
nothing more suggestive than a blank sheet of paper.
Anything can happen there. This, then, is my task, and I
feel it always has been: to transform the everyday into
magic, the real into fantasy, the vulgar into beauty.
Sometimes I think I've succeeded, though not often, but at
least I've tried. When they let me, that is, because for
reasons I still don't understand, some people are annoyed,
enraged, or even frightened by fantasy.

In any case, I belong to that group of people who, in
Antonio Machado's words, "won everything and lost
everything." And here I am. Could I be an image in a
dream?

Don Maitz

Don Maitz received his art education at the University of Hartford Art School and graduated at the top of his class at the Paier School of Art. As an illustrator he has created over seventy-five paperback jackets, artwork for *Marvel Comics*, portraits, landscapes, and advertising for New York agencies and several national firms. Maitz's artwork has been featured in art galleries and exhibits, including the 22nd Annual Exhibit of the Society of Illustrators, at which he won a Silver Medal. Among his other accomplishments is receiving the H. P. Lovecraft Award for Best Artist at the 6th World Fantasy Convention in 1980.

"In becoming a visual artist, I found myself faced with dilemmas. What subjects to realize—portraits, landscapes, still lifes, or abstracts? In what form should the subjects be represented—drawings, paintings, sculpture, or collage? How should I approach the subject—impressionistically, realistically, surrealistically, or abstractly?

"Through experimentation I found I enjoyed all of the above and could not make a choice as to which particular art form to claim as my own. I decided to enter a field where all of the above could be subjected to my discretion. I attempt to show with conviction the furthest reaches of my imagination with whatever materials suit the occasion. The experience is often an enjoyable one, and if my enjoyment is communicated to the viewer, then I feel the artwork is a success.

"Calling myself a fantasy illustrator, by definition, means that I am explaining—exemplifying imagination unrestrained by reality. My goal is to entertain visually, to produce a fantastic scene where make believe, pretend, and 'what if' run free. Illustrating the book jackets of fantastic stories calls for reflecting the nature of an author's ideas in a visually refreshing manner so that someone looking for diversion from the day-to-day routine will have, at a glance, some idea of the book's content and be entertained at the same time."

Carlos Ochagavia

Born in Spain and educated in Argentina, Carlos Ochagavia came to New York when he was awarded a scholarship to study with Morris Kantor at the Art Students League. When he returned to Argentina, he specialized in etchings, serigraphics, and paintings, receiving several awards for his work. Among his other artwork are several murals and illustrations for limited editions of books.

Carlos Ochagavia's interest in film inspired him to create several short subject and animated films, one of which won a Mention in the French festivals of Annecy and Tours. In 1964 he participated in the Venice Festival of film in advertising.

In 1974 Ochagavia left Argentina and came to the United States to continue his illustrations. His works are on permanent exhibition at the Museo Nacional de Bellas Artes and the Museo Nacional del Grabado in Buenos Aires. Over the years he has also staged one-man shows of his art and participated in many group shows in Argentina

"I was born on this planet, more exactly, in the land of Don Quixote, and in the same way he saw life in the windmills, I see it in the outer space.

"Thanks to my interest in painting and to my art studies in Spain, Argentina, and New York, I can have the fun of doing science fiction illustrations."

Kenneth Distler

Science fiction literature has always held a fascination for me and though I read avidly othe subjects, it is always with great pleasure when I can escape into faraway worlds where reality an fantasy merge, and one becomes visually involved in those alien landscapes. This kind of involvement helps me to create an illustration by totally losing myself in the mood of the story. Everything around me disappears and the words on paper transform themselves into moving pictures in my head. Therefore, my first approach to creating an illustration is in knowing the story and its atmosphere.

Having chosen a scene that attracts me strongly and tha can be interpreted most effectively into a picture, I now work loosely on small scraps of paper, transferring thoughts into abstract patterns of lights and darks with a broad flat pencil. When I'm satisfied with the planning and arranging of the picture-making components in a given area, I set this paper before me and work on composing the picture in realism. I do this with plastic models. These models don't necessarily have anything to do with my subject pictorially. They are merely a device for light and shade, and simulate as closely as possible the action I want to develop. I then begin to arrange and redraw these models so that they fit the time and place of the event occurring in the story. This is visual story writing and a very direct approach to composition. At the end of this stage I prepare a color sketch for approval, and then take i to a photographic studio. The final stage of the illustration is when I transfer all my ideas into a finished project.

In addition to science fiction, other subjects I like to paint are children, Westerns, and romance. I also have several outside interests—the most important one is horses. I own a six-year-old Registered Quarter Horse chestnut, named Moriah's Beau, who has been with me for the past two years. During my spare time I am training him for Western Pleasure classes for horse shows. We have won many ribbons and some trophies.

84

James Z. Yost

When I was five I turned over a rotted log in the woods, and to my amazement there was revealed underneath an Alien Environment. Even then I thought "Ah, here is my Home!"

So I've been searching for Home since that time, making images of such Familiar Places, and most important, telling visual stories of the people who live there.

For after all, people is what science fiction is really about; not laser-ray guns, quantum mechanics, and interstellar spaceships. These are just the props and the stage upon which science fiction is acted. The beauty of *good* science fiction is that it gets to the heart, to the essence of human drama and lets it unfold free from all the Tedious Limitations of the "real" world. Oops, back to Earth . . .

One day while my drama was unfolding I became aware of the Tedious Limitations of Suburbia, and decided to look for Home elsewhere. I had to find someplace different, bizarre, really alien. So naturally I packed my black leather picnic basket and moved all starry-eyed to New York City.

Now New York *is* science fiction in that you find such an insane juxtaposition of incredibly different beings and experiential universes all co-existing in more or less the same physical space. Here people create their *own* reality. I think it's just wonderful, me being a country boy and having Rolena, Queen of the Green Galaxy, for a next-door neighbor.

Anyway, that's the way it is; so to quote what some semifamous person once said so appropriately, "I paint what I see."